Eric Red

Strange Fruit

Evil Jester Press

New York

Cover art and interior illustrations
by Gary McCluskey, copyright © 2014

Edited by David C. Hayes
Formatted by Peter Giglio

First Edition: April 2014

ISBN: 978-0692201947

Printed in the United States and the United Kingdom

The carnies came in the quiet cool before dawn.

The town was still sleeping, houses and stores dark, streets devoid of traffic as the carnival drove through. A traveling caravan of trucks, trailers and double-wides lumbered in shadowed procession down the main drag. Tires left tread marks rolling over one of the fallen posters announcing the carnival's arrival that workers had put up around town days before. They set up on the field at the outskirts while it was still dark, pulling in the vehicles and offloading the tents.

Hammers, electric drills and cranking chains reverberated across the lonely fairgrounds as a portable radio played a country song against the drone of the crickets. In the stark flare of the headlights from the silhouetted trucks, lanky and unshaven hobo carnies with long hair, stoned eyes and tattoos on brown dull skin milled around like ants setting up the fairway rides and booths. The men looked like derelicts but they knew what they were doing. They cranked the winches that raised the carousel. They plugged in the generators. They drove up and unhitched the trailers. The air smelled of wet soil, rust, oil and fresh coffee. Gradually, the crickets stopped chirping as a rooster crowed. The shadowy obstructions of the spectral tents and carnival rides rose fantastically against the stars. Soon, the sky lightened over the

Ferris wheel and Loop-The-Loop. The roadies dispersed. It had been a long night's load-out, drive and load-in, time to catch a few hours sleep before the locals arrived for the evening festivities. The city of Lee, Alabama, was just another name on the map, another whistle stop for them.

Clyde Dodd and Butch McCauley stepped right up. Calliope music filled the warm night air. They bought their tickets at the kiosk with the garish bright light bulbs at the fenced perimeter of the carnival that filled the fairground with activity, machinery and contraptions. The ticket booth housed the fat lady with the white and purple clown makeup and glitter sparkling on her sagging skin, a cigarette dangling from her lips. The two boys were 17. Clyde had blonde and blue eyed all-

American good looks and was well put together. Butch was bland and unremarkable in appearance, his eyes set too far apart. Tonight, the high school football players wore matching blue and yellow varsity jackets with the Bulldog mascot patch. Both felt the same cheap, visceral excitement in the air as each swigged from a brown-bagged pint of Jack Daniels and toked off a joint, suitably jacked up to enjoy the carnival. This was no typical Saturday night what with the carnival in town.

"Hold a sec. Gotta drain the snake." Butch, nervous, looked both ways as the drunk Clyde swaggered to the gear box of the Merry Go Round, unzipped, whipped it out with both hands and pissed a figure eight with a satisfied groan.

Butch, not wanting to get arrested, nervously kept a lookout for cops or angry carnies. "Would you hurry it up? There's people all over the place."

"You want to hold it for me?" Clyde made a show of groaning with relief and shaking his thing, before stuffing it back in his jeans and sidling up to Butch. "You're just jealous. C'mon, let's find some pussy." The teen boys passed under the Ferris Wheel, staring up at the flying skirts of some of the chicks as they were swept high into the vertiginous sky by the towering ride. Butch tried to act macho and said he was up for some of that.

"Don't worry. I'll give you some of my sloppy seconds," Clyde chided his pal.

They rounded the ride and entered onto the fairway, the smell of stale cotton candy and hot butter assaulting their nostrils, the bustling place so packed with locals it looked like half the town had turned out tonight. Calliope music blasted out of tinny speakers on a midway bright with pulsing neon light. Tacky souvenir and hot dog stands were surrounded by kids. Young couples manned the rifle and water gun games, the boys trying to win the girls prizes. A clown lumbered past, reeking of booze. A rusted Bumper Cars ride jostled and banged, as dinged and decrepit fiberglass buggies careened off each other. It all became a happy blur to Clyde and Butch, the more they passed the bottle. Down the midway, in a darkening corner past the lights of the rides and attractions, sat a large tent. The boys ventured down the grassy walkway between the food vendors, into the shadows towards the tent as if drawn by a mysterious force. They stood at the entrance to the Sideshow. It was a big tent, a hundred yards wide. A large gaudy canvas banner covered the front of the tent with wild colorful storybook paintings of the human and animal oddities promised inside.

"*SEE: THE TWO-HEADED COW! ALL LIVE!*"

"*SEE: THE ALLIGATOR MAN!*"

"*SEE: THE HUMAN TRUNK! NATURE'S ARMLESS LEGLESS MAN!*"

"*SEE: THE SIAMESE TWIN SISTERS SADIE AND ROSE!*"

"*SEE: THE GEEK! FREAK OF NATURE!*"

"*ALL REAL! ALL ALIVE!*"

Butch felt his stomach lurch with a queasy mixture of fascination and revulsion. "Dude." Clyde took a sip of the Jack, wiped his lips with the back of his hand and passed the brown bag to his pal. "I am so up for this."

Fear of what was inside the tent, something Butch could already feel, lurked too close for comfort, made his stomach clench. It lay just beyond the flap of the entrance, just a few more steps ahead. He could smell the straw inside. The canvas. The sweat. The strangeness. The freaks. "I hate freaks," Butch blurted, disgusted how lame those words sounded soon as they left his mouth.

"Pussy."

"Eat me." Just to show Clyde, Butch ducked through the opening of the tent first.

The bull stood behind a fence on a bed of straw, normal from the neck down. The second head grew out of the side of the first on a thick leathery neck. Its four eyes lolled with bovine stupidity under the four horns of its grotesquely misshapen head. The snout was cleft into two. Drool poured out of both lazy mouths, one set of teeth munching straw lazily as the other jaws chewed its cud. The yellowed teeth were distorted in distended, deformed gums.

The massive twin skulls of the steer weighed heavily on its mangy body. Its tail swished casually at flies. Butch followed Clyde up to the fenced in pen, trying not to show his apprehension. The younger boy had the sense they had trespassed somewhere damned and forbidden in the close recesses of the tent. Cow dander and dung filled his nostrils. A local farmer in overalls and jeans stood beside them, already at the pen. Butch recognized him as Lewis, somebody who lived on the edge of town. Sometimes he came to the games. The farmer winked at the boys.

"Bet you ain't gonna eat a hamburger again soon, eh Clyde? Good game last Saturday, hero."

"Thanks, Mister." The man left.

Suddenly, a disgusting deep wheezing, thick with mucous and crud, sounded inside the tent. Butch whirled to see the two-headed cow struggling to catch its breath. It had something caught in its throat. Both sets of eyes bulged white and horrid in the double skull, tongues engorged in both mouths. Clyde busted up and laughed cruelly at the scene. But Butch looked on with slack-jawed horror, mortified by the spectacle. The freak cow tossed its deformed twin heads to and fro, choking, stomping its hooves, and smashing its shoulders into the wooden slats of the pen. Immediately, a flash of movement occurred in back of the tent as something small and quick ducked under the rear canvas flap. A little dwarf with a sunken face and cauliflower nose slipped under the stall and crawled with lighting speed up the side of the cow's belly, his diminutive arms and legs clambering over the neck and spine of the steer onto the top of its cleft skull. The midget stuck his arm right into the mouth of one of the heads and reached up to the shoulder down its gullet. Making a squinting expression of extreme exertion and distaste, the dwarf yanked out a fistful of clogged straw. He dropped off the two-headed cow that gasped for breath, and washed his arms in a water bucket. Both teenagers watched speechless. The midget waddled off on two stubby legs to the edge of the tent, and then turned and shot a glance of such malice and resentment to the boys they both took a step back. The dwarf flipped them the bird, then ducked back under the edge of the tent and was gone. Exchanging wild glances, Clyde and Butch laughed nervously. They left the stall and entered the next section of the tent.

The two boys stopped dead in their tracks when they saw The Siamese twins.

The girls were beautiful. Both twins looked in their teens. They sat on a sofa on a wooden truss, dressed in skimpy bikinis, which showed off their identical hourglass figures. Both had long black hair that tumbled over gentle shoulders and soft and perfectly pale freckled skin. Sensually built and full bosomed, their breasts were high and firm, their sculpted rear ends round and saucy. Small waists led to a not ungraceful conjoined section of their lower hips, a bar of flesh, above the curvy swell of their backsides as both sat with legs crossed at an adjacent angle to one another. Both girls winked at the boys. One of them blew a gum bubble, as they returned their attention to a book one was reading and a portable television set the other watched.

Clyde leaned close to Butch's face as they ogled the semi-nude twin sisters. He whispered in his ear. "Dude, those babes are hotter than any chicks in Lee."

Butch nodded in agreement. "Let's talk to them."

"Who's who?" Clyde asked the girls.

"I'm Sadie."

"I'm Rose."

"You're beautiful."

"Thank you."

"You're hot."

Butch couldn't believe it but he was getting wood. Sadie uncurled one leg and crossed her knee over the other. The boy got a brief glimpse of a tuft of black public hair under the bush bulge of her bikini. "Do you have a DQ around here?" Sadie said. "I love their Mud Slides."

"There's a Carvel in the next town," said
Clyde.

"Sure is hot on a night like this. I could
use a Hurricane." Sadie batted her eyes at

them. "I was thinking of going after the show."

"Your sister like a sundae?" Butch asked.

"I don't know Rose, you like a sundae?"

Rose's nose was buried in a romance novel. "I got to watch my weight."

"Don't you mean *our* weight?"

Rose winked at Sadie, who rolled her eyes in exasperation. "Rose would rather have her nose stuck in that book than live life, but *I* like to *live* life." A fan was blowing. The girls took chunks from an ice chest and cooled their foreheads and necks as water droplets dibbled down their shoulders and breasts.

"I think you're prettier than any girls in town." Clyde turned on the charm.

Butch eagerly interjected. "Me too. I mean, I agree you're prettier than them.

Hell, you're prettier than anybody around here," he babbled.

"Which of us?"

"Both of you."

"You're sweet. Aren't they sweet, Rose?"

"They're both sweet. So what are you boys' names?"

"I'm Clyde. This is Butch."

"You both play football."

"He's quarterback. I'm a linebacker."

"Bet you both have girlfriends, don't you?"

Butch felt eyes on the back of his head and turned.

The dwarf was glaring at them from the recesses of the tent. His lips smeared flat in his toothless mouth, he retracted into the gloom.

"You girls got boyfriends?" Clyde asked, sidling up to the edge of the wooden platform the Siamese twins perched on.

"Sometimes," said Sadie.

"No we don't," said Rose.

"We do. Did. Back in Kentucky last month."

"They wasn't boyfriends. Not really. They was just friends." Rose returned her gaze to the trash paperback.

Glancing at his friend, Butch saw Clyde give him The Look. They'd employed The Look since junior high, using it on the field and off it with girls. The Look meant get ready to make a play. But right then, a group of new customers filtered in, and the girls turned their fresh attentions and peculiar charms to them. The boys reluctantly had to move on to the next attraction. The sullen dwarf was at their ankles, pig eyes flinty, making impatient gestures with his little wax ball hands for them to scram.

They passed through the opening of the tent, into the smell of canvas and urine. The painted green letters above the cage were enhanced with dripping wax. Two lurid words... *"THE GEEK."* Then below... "Do Not Feed or Tease!"

The Geek was the victim of an unimaginable birth defect. His head was huge and elephantine, bulbous folds of flesh billowing out the side of a malformed skull on a scrawny, contorted body. He wore huge blue jeans that had a hole cut out of the back for the spinal vestigial tail. His feet were troll's trotters. A large eye, inches lower than the other, gazed out at the boys in a soup of pain. He stank. Clyde let out a scream when he got an eyeful of the freak. Butch's stomach curdled at the sight of the Geek, but his pal actually shrieked like a girl which made Butch laugh real hard. Drunk and embarrassed at his unmanly outburst, Clyde whirled angrily on his smirking friend, but Butch couldn't help it and laughed harder. Then the boy noticed the midget pointing at him from about three feet off the sawdust floor, cackling in ridicule. "Hey shut the fuck up!" he yelled at the dwarf, who jumped up and down, chortling derisively. The teenager made a violent move towards the cackling little person, who scuttled into the next tent. The shamed Geek covered his face, mumbled, and drew back into the shadows. Still smarting from his humiliation, Clyde pushed Butch away and turned his attentions to the human oddity in the cage. "Hey handsome." The Geek got to his feet. "C'mere." Clyde smiled warmly. "It's okay, man." He held out the pint of Jack Daniels in the brown paper bag.

Butch looked at Clyde in alarm. "What are you doing, asshole?" Too late. The Geek, actually forming something resembling a faintly human smile in mouth full of missing teeth, reached gratefully for the bottle. Clyde meanly yanked it away. The Geek looked crestfallen. The kid spit cruelly in its face. The freak was spattered with saliva. It screamed. It pulled its hair. It ran around the cage in hysterical, idiot circles. High-pitched shrieks of alarm escaped its throat. Four fingered hands gripped the bars and shook it like an ape. "What the fuck are you doing, man?" Butch felt disgusted and shamed.

"They're freaks. They're used to it."

"Don't be a jerk."

Clyde taunted the Geek. Spat at it again. And again until the miserable wretch crawled into the back of the cage and covered its head with its arms.

The click of a hammer cocked back on a gun stopped the cruel hijinks. "Get the fuck out." Clyde and Butch turned to see the midget holding a .44 Magnum snub-nosed revolver in both hands. It looked bigger than his head. And it was aimed at their balls.

The boys fled.

There hadn't been a murder in Lee. Not in his lifetime.

Until now.

Sheriff Danny Girdler steered his police Plymouth through the flat, dark ribbon of blacktop. Mosquitoes swept past the headlights of his Plymouth. He was 35, born and raised in Lee. He'd been in law enforcement since he was 17 back when his father had been Sheriff. A heart attack had felled Danny senior five years ago and the well-liked son had won the job easily in the local election. Mostly things were quiet around here. Lee was a peaceful town. Population 653. Everybody knew one another. Had grown up together. The townspeople were his friends, they were nice folks and his was mostly a quiet job. That's why his head swam and stomach lurched with the news he received 22 minutes ago in the middle of the night.

The locals had found the body. Two teenaged sons of a local farmer named Jenkins had been camping out on the bank of the Indian River. One had gone to the shore to take a piss and saw the corpse in the rapids. Their father had called Girdler. The cop told them to stay at the scene and not touch anything, saying he would be out there in a half hour. Two questions ran around Sheriff Girdler's head as he put the pedal to the metal.

Who the hell?

And why the fuck?

Up ahead, he saw the dirt turnoff onto Jenkins property and swung a left. His car jounced over the gravely two-track road. Dust filled the windshield, obstructing his vision. Then ahead, he saw the flashlight beams flaring through the trees near the riverbank. The cop pulled up his car and parked. He grabbed his hat and braced himself for what he was about to see, surprised by his apprehension. Girdler took a deep breath, and got out of the vehicle. He headed down to the riverbank where the three silhouettes of the farmer and his sons stood with the flashlight, waving him on with the beam. "Over here, Sheriff!"

He saw it right away. The body lay half washed ashore, soaked with water and blood. Girdler unhooked the flashlight from his belt and knelt by the wet stones. His belly tightening, he shone the beam over the corpse. It was a young male. Hadn't been dead long. Hours at most. The body had been hacked and slashed with what looked like multiple knife wounds. The face was barely recognizable, having taken the brunt of the slashing, the ragged flesh hanging loose around the right cheek and jaw, the nose half sheared off and an eyeball gouged from an empty socket. Bone and tendon, swollen with water, hung in rags around the ugly gashes. Identification would be easy. The football jacket was the Bulldogs. Girdler rubbed his eyes. "Oh boy," he sighed under his breath.

It was one of the local kids and this was going to be a shit show.

The Sheriff had a good idea it was Clyde Dodd even before he pulled the wallet out of the sopping jeans and found the DMV learner's permit with the teen's name on it. Girdler recognized the long blonde hair and the general physical build of the popular local high school football player from the games he'd seen. He picked up

Dodd several times for drunk and disorderly behavior and the cop privately found the popular kid to be a cocky punk who got away with a lot of crap because he scored touchdowns. But Dodd had really pissed off somebody this time. Somebody who had gone hog wild on him with a big sharp knife. The stab wounds had a psychotic clumsy fury about them. Wracking his brain, pumped by the sudden realization he had his first murder case on his hands, Girdler tried to list suspects. Who around here could Dodd have angered enough to do this to him? A dumped ex-girlfriend? No, there were no girls capable of murder in town. An enemy student? No, the boy was very well liked at school. Clyde got into a few fights but so did a lot of kids. Nobody from around here would do this. Lee was a dull town. Folks knew each other. Grew up together. Lee was normal. Whoever did this killing was...

Different.

The Sheriff stood and looked out into the deep black country darkness. Far off in the distance, the tiny jewel colored neon lights of the carnival glittered in the fairground fields like a landed alien spaceship.

He knew in his gut.

Whoever killed Dodd wasn't local. And wasn't normal.

How do you tell a family their child has been killed? He didn't know, but he was going to find out. While he drove, Sheriff Girdler raised his Deputy on the radio, a 60-year old man named Abner Ross who worked for his dad and now him. The voice on the radio was bleary with sleep. And probably drunk. "Yeah?"

"Wake up. We got a killing on our hands. One of the local kids. Clyde Dodd."

"You're shitting me. How?"

"Looks like a knifing. A real bad one. They found him in the river out at the Jenkins farm. I'm out on 43 heading out to the family's house to tell the parents and I'm not looking forward to it."

"Want me there?"

"No. I need you finding out who last saw the kid and who he was with last night. Think the killers could be local?"

"Hell no."

"Me neither. Gotta be someone with that carnival out at the fairground. We're going to have to detain the whole damn carnival within city limits and question every last one of them. It's going to be a long day." The Sheriff hung up the radio as he saw the mailbox for the Dodd's house glint in the distance in his headlights. He turned up the driveway and parked in front of the ranch home. It was still an hour before dawn. The lights in the farmhouse were off, but there was a lamp burning in the barn. Ernie Dodd, Clyde's father, would be up. He was a big, white haired, hard-nosed farmer who happened to be the local football coach. The lawman got out of the squad car. "Mr. Dodd?"

"Sheriff." The father stepped out of the barn and lost his smile quick when he saw the look on the cop's face. "What's wrong?"

"It's about Clyde." Girdler took off his hat, and immediately wished he had done so before he spoke. He'd never dealt with a murder, never dealt with telling the family about the death of a loved one, he didn't want to do it, didn't want to be here, but it was his job and it was his responsibility.

Suck it up, he heard his father's voice in his head tell him. Ernie Dodd just watched him curiously.

"I'm sorry, Mr. Dodd. Your boy's been killed. We found the body an hour ago. I'm so sorry." The big man just stood for what seemed like endless minutes, blank and impassive, watching Girdler and blinking, just blinking, as a terrible shudder quivered his large figure like a palsy until it rocked Dodd, a tree in a hurricane. He tried to form words but his lips just trembled. Then he fell against the fence and screamed his lungs out, screaming and screaming, until his throat was raw and his voice trailed to a squeal. Damn, thought the Sheriff. This was worse than he thought it would be. The swinging door of the front porch flew open and Ernie's wife, Pam, burst out onto the porch, responding to the screams, her face filled with fear at the sight of her husband and the cop. "Ernie! Sheriff! W-What's wrong?"

Damn.

Damn.

Sheriff Girdler sat in the Sheriff's office across his desk from Butch McCauley. It was 7:23 AM. He had gotten to his office in town after leaving the Dodd place just after the sun came up. Deputy Ross had been there making calls since 5:00 AM and learned a farmer named Sam Lewis had placed Clyde Dodd with his friend Butch McCauley at the sideshow at around 11:15 PM the night before. That was good enough for Girdler. The carnival would be detained within city limits. The two cops planned to drive over to the fairgrounds as soon as they finished questioning Butch. The teen sat slumped in the chair, hung over and sullen. "Let's go over it again." Girdler leaned back in his chair. "You said you and Clyde split up after you left the sideshow."

"Yeah."

"I thought you guys drove in together."

"No, we each took our own cars."

"Did Clyde get into any fights with anyone last night?"

"Nope. Not while he was with me. We was just at the carnival having a good time."

"You talk to anybody?"

The kid shrugged.

"What does that mean?"

"No. Nobody."

"Not Sam Lewis. The farmer. He talked to both you boys in the sideshow."

"Oh yeah, him."

"Yeah, him."

"Want a cool drink, Butch?" Deputy Ross indicated the water cooler. The kid nodded and started to get up but the man gestured him to sit. "I got it," Said Ross as he fetched a clean glass from the cabinet, held it by the edge, filled it at the cooler and then brought it to Butch. The kid took the glass in his hand and took a thirsty drink. Danny Girdler eyed the young football player across his desk, but the kid wasn't making eye contact. "You seem all torn up about your pal." The Sheriff tossed a glance to his Deputy, who also seemed perplexed by the boy's odd demeanor.

"It sucks."

"Especially for him."

"Guess it ain't hit me yet."

"You own a knife, Butch?" Girdler leaned forward.

"What kind of knife?"

"Own one?"

Butch scratched his elbow. "Sure. Who doesn't?"

"Can I see it?"

"What?"

"Can. I. See. It?"

"I don't have it."

"Where is it?"

"I lost it."

Then the Sheriff lost it. Hammering his fist on the desk, scattering pencils, he got the boy's fearful attention at last. "Listen dumbass!" the cop shouted. "Your friend was murdered last night! You were the last person seen with him! He was knifed and now you sit here and tell me you lost your knife! You better start takin' this whole situation a hell of a lot more seriously or I'm gonna break your ass!"

Suddenly, Butch broke down and cried. He sat there and bawled and bawled.

Girdler exchanged confused glances with Ross.

What the hell happened last night?

The two cops drove out the carnival in distracted silence. "That boy Butch isn't telling us something," The Sheriff told his Deputy.

"No shit."

"Noticed you took his prints off the glass he was drinking from in the office."

"Figure you keep me around for something."

Parking in front of the carnival main gate at the fairground, Sheriff Girdler got out with Deputy Ross. They squinted against the hot, dry southern heat and walked up to the ticket booth. "We need to speak to who's in charge of this operation."

The Fat Lady sucked on her Lucky Strike. "That would be Mr. Stitch."

Minutes later, a thin, wiry figure in denims walked bow legged towards them in cowboy boots and a cowboy hat. Tattoos and scars showed around his neck. His jeans sported a moose knuckle bulge beneath a heavy silver and turquoise belt buckle. The man wore mirrored Ray Ban shades, had a face like leather and was of an indeterminate age past fifty. He offered his hand with long spindly fingers that closed like a spider around Girdler's when they shook. "I'm Stitch. I manage the carnival."

"There was a murder last night. Did you know about that?"

"No, sir, I sure didn't."

"Local boy."

"Sorry to hear it."

Girdler showed a photo of Clyde Dodd to Stitch, whose mirrored Ray Bans reflected a distorted image, but the man shook his head when asked if he recognized the boy. Further questions about the carnival being the last place the kid was seen or if the manager knew of any trouble got no response. Stitch just watched him. Girdler was getting annoyed watching his reflection in the Stitch's mirrored shades, so he didn't say anything, and let his silence do some reflecting of its own back at the carnie. It worked. The man spoke. "My people don't want trouble. Don't cause none either. That's how we stay in business. And all our permits are in order."

"Well, Mr. Stitch, this whole area is now an official crime scene and this is a murder investigation. I'm going to have to detain your carnival and everyone in it within city limits for the next few days at least. That includes you. My Deputy and I are going to have to question everybody that works here."

"Sheriff, we got a schedule to keep. We're due at the Harrisburg, Kentucky, fairground this Friday."

"There's nothing I can do about that."

"We got a living to make."

"Yeah, well, I got a local boy who ain't living at all. And he was last seen here."

"You can't do this."

"Sure I can. Can lock up every one of you people in jail downtown during this process, or you can stop giving me shit and cooperate."

"We'll cooperate."

"Damn straight. I'll be doing the questioning and taking statements at the Sheriff's office in Lee. Right across from the town square. Get your people, all of 'em, down there in two hours." The local cops turned their back on Mr. Stitch and walked back to the car.

The Sheriff looked at his Deputy. "Ross, stick around just make sure nobody leaves town." Swinging behind the wheel, Danny Girdler drove out of the pasture back onto the main road.

The receding reflection of the patrol car getting swallowed in dust was reflected in Mr. Stitch's shades as he stood impassively watching the cop leave. He spat tobacco juice on the ground as the stale sun beat down. Deputy Ross leaned against the pole, arms crossed, watching him.

Flies buzzed as the day grew hotter.

By noon the town was full of freaks.

They were in the diner. They sat in the park. They wandered the sidewalks. The town didn't like it. Not one bit. On Main Street, a yellow school bus lumbered by. Inside, the children gawked at the human oddities on the sidewalk of their town. Several first graders screamed and cried at the sight of the disfigured and misshapen folks, while others laughed and pointed and made faces. The freaks glared back at the bus.

Sheriff Girdler was just entering his office when Mayor Bob Driggs collared him. The overweight old politician looked distressed. "What are all these freaks doing in town, Danny? It's upsetting everybody."

"Because I'm questioning them at my office about Clyde Dodd's killing, why the hell do you think?"

"Couldn't you have questioned them out at the fairground? That's where they belong. They're scaring people."

"I question suspects in the police station, Bob, because one, it's where I have my files and my computer and my coffee pot, and two, I don't have to explain myself to you."

Mr. Stitch stood outside the door of the police station in front of a line of carnies and freaks stretching down the block. Girdler brushed past the mayor and entered his office where Deputy Ross was already sitting behind his desk talking to the Human Trunk. The room was filled with brightly colored carnival folk. By noon, the cops had interviewed half the carnival. The dwarf had said the boys were behaving aggressively, but none of the other carnival people had witnessed any altercations. They all backed one another up. All of the carnies were eyewitnesses on where the other carnies were throughout the evening.

"These carnival people stick tighter than glue." Ross sighed.

"We ain't interviewed everybody yet. Nobody's leaving town until I get some answers," Girdler said. "I'm going across the street and getting some coffee." Girdler walked out the door, tipping his hat to the crowd of townspeople that gathered across the street in the park. He did not get the usual smiles in return and the many hard stares made the cop uncomfortable as he crossed Main Street to Joe's Diner.

When he entered the restaurant, a ceiling fan slowly turned in the humid heat and the jukebox was quiet. Inside, at the end of the booths, sat the alligator man and the bearded lady. The dwarf sat across from them. Other town regulars were giving them a wide berth, sitting at the other end of the diner. Girdler walked up to Sam, the owner, and ordered two coffees. "Do these people have to be here?" The proprietor asked.

"Your sign says 'No Shoes No Shirts No Service' Sam. Looks to me like these folks have both."

The two Siamese twins, Rose and Sadie, sat side by side in one of the booths. The table covered their physical conjoinment and, for the casual observer, they were just the two prettiest girls in the town sitting side by side. Rose shot a sweet, unaffected glance to Girdler and he returned a grin, tipping his hat. Grabbing his coffees, he walked over to the booth. "Mind if I join you?"

"Please sit down, Sheriff."

"Call me Danny."

Rose smiled. "Looks like we're causing quite the fuss."

Girdler looked over the sisters' shoulders to the dwarf in the next booth arguing with the waitress, Stella.

"Excuse me, we ordered our eggs a half an hour ago," the high voice piped. She clearly did not like serving freaks.

"I gave the order to the cook," the waitress replied coldly giving the cop a distressed look as she brushed by.

"We're so sorry what happened to that boy," Sadie said. "He come by our tent last night with his friend and they both seemed nice." She nudged Rose, who stared into her coffee. "Wasn't that right, Rose?"

"Sure was."

"I hear he got shot."

Rose looked at Sadie, then down into her coffee.

"Stabbed actually," Girdler quietly corrected her.

"Sheriff, ain't nobody in the carnival that's violent or would hurt folks." Rose spoke up with strain in her voice. "We're the nicest people. We just look different. Do you think somebody in our carnival done it?"

"I have to question everyone, ma'am, it's just routine."

"I see."

Girdler looked at Rose and Sadie. "So what do you ladies think of our little town?"

"Nice."

"Nice."

"They're all nice towns." Rose sighed winsomely. "But we never stay long in any of 'em."

"Most of them, you're not missing much," the cop smiled.

"We wouldn't know."

"That sounds lonesome."

"We have each other."

Girdler looked at the girls, thinking never was a truer word spoken. He studied their faces for a moment. Their features were almost exactly the same, both had pretty heart-shaped faces, but there were differences. Rose had a genuine guilelessness and warmth in her eyes, a wide-eyed innocent stare that looked away shyly a lot. Sadie had the same naiveté, but there was a mischievous glint in her eyes and she held his gaze boldly. It seemed like Sadie had a few lines around her eyes. The intimate bond and love connection between the two Siamese twins was tangible. The Sheriff decided he'd never met anyone like them. "You both know how lucky you are?" he said.

"How so?"

"You'll never be alone."

"We know. If one of us died the other one would, too."

"You have nice eyes, Sheriff. Doesn't he have nice eyes, Sadie?"

"He does."

"Kind."

"Intelligent."

Rose whispered in Sadie's ear. Girdler couldn't hear. Sadie nodded. Rose looked at him. "Sheriff, would you like to stop by the trailer sometime? We know you're busy but we make good coffee."

"I'd like that."

"Seeing as we ain't going no place for right now's anyway."

"Not for now."

"Here's our number." Rose scribbled it on a napkin and handed it to the cop.

Girder turned his head to a commotion happening outside the window across the street by the Sheriff's station. There were a growing mob of townspeople gathered around the carnies on the sidewalk, and voices were raised. The lawman grabbed his hat.

"If you'll excuse me, ladies."

Bursting out the door, Girdler rushed across the street to where the people were crowding and hoped he wasn't too late. Ernie Dodd paced the sidewalk in front of the line of carnival workers who were waiting on the sidewalk to be questioned. He flashed a printed out class photo of his handsome dead son smiling in his football jersey at the line of freaks, as tears poured down his face. "See him? This was Clyde! He was my boy! He was just 17!"

The town had his back. Several local parents flanked him.

The carnies cringed and stared back, tight with tension.

"He was bad!" The Geek blurted. "He got what was coming!"

Dodd whirled on the human oddity. "What did you say?"

"He was bad! He hurt me! He got what was coming to him!"

"*You sonofabitch you killed my boy!*" The embittered father exploded, and throwing his beefy hands around the Geek's neck, he slammed the freak against the building and beat his misshapen skull against the brick wall. Stitch, the alligator man and two tattooed carnies leapt on the embittered father, struggling to yank him off. Dodd was apoplectic with rage, veins bulging on his neck as he pummeled the freak. *"You killed him didn't you?"*

The protesting Geek screeched in a hideous high-pitched wail.

A few townsmen rushed to the aid of their fellow citizen and grabbed the carnies. Then all hell broke loose. Fists flew. Voices rose. It turned into a riot. Ross was inside the office when he saw the mad rush of bodies surging past the windows outside and, upon hearing the screams and shouts, he grabbed his pump shotgun and was out the door. Girdler joined him and the two cops waded into a sea of flying fists and kicking legs as the local townspeople attacked the carnies and the carnival workers and freaks fought right back. The Sheriff yelled for everyone to break it up, heaving people this way and that with his bare hands.

Then the crowd suddenly backed off.

The dwarf had drawn his .44 and was shielding the Geek, holding the attackers at bay. "*I not kill nobody,*" the Geek bawled.

The Sheriff instantly drew his .357 and fell to a combat crouch, aiming the muzzle between the midget's eyes.

"Drop the gun!" He shouted. The dwarf kept his grip on the big wooden stock of the shiny black cannon, his piglet eyes flashing with confusion and panic. Then he felt the barrel of Ross' .12 gauge shotgun tickling the side of his face and heard the hammer cock. The Deputy snarled for him to drop his weapon or lose his head. The dwarf's Magnum clattered to the pavement. "Cuff him," snarled Girdler, who whirled around on the mob of townspeople. "Clear out of here! All of you!"

"You gonna arrest that freak, Danny?" Dodd faced Girdler. "He said he killed my boy! Everybody heard it!"

"I said no such thing and I didn't kill nobody," the Geek wailed.

The Sheriff told his Deputy to take them inside and Ross led the freaks out of the line of fire.

"You go home, Ernie, and you let us do our jobs." Girdler told Dodd and then turned to face the crowd. "All of you people get out of here." The cop stood and watched the town disperse, registering the brutal expressions in their eyes he hadn't seen before. Suddenly he felt very alone. He didn't like the feeling.

A half hour later the cops had questioned the Geek. The half man said he'd been harassed by Clyde but never left his cage. Nobody there that night disputed his statement. The dwarf got a night in the holding cell. By late afternoon all of the carnies had been questioned. The lawmen called it a day.

No arrests had been made.

The killer was still out there.

The following afternoon, Butch McCauley was walking Shirley Roberts home from school on the side of the road into town. Clyde's girl had some nice tits, cannonballs slung in her bra under her tight cheerleader sweater, with her strawberry hair that smelt so fine. Shirl had wanted to talk a lot since her boyfriend got murdered two nights ago; there were lots of tears and Butch made sure he was the shoulder to cry on. He peered over and watched the swells of her buttocks pumping in her tight jeans as they walked. So fine. In a few days, he was going to get to first base.

"Clyde was a jerk, I don't know why I miss him so much," she said softly, staring at the sky.

"He was my best friend. I miss him, too."

"You're really nice, Butch, you know that? I never noticed it before."

Butch had sure noticed Shirl. In fact, he wanted her so much he ached with resentful jealousy when he and Clyde would double date and those two would be making out, Shirl all over his friend. They should have gotten a room. All he could think of during those double dates was not his own girl but what Shirl looked like naked. Mostly he wanted Shirl because Clyde had her. But she was with Clyde and he couldn't compete. She'd be humping that lucky asshole at every available opportunity. But not anymore.

"I feel so close to you," Shirl sighed, resting her head on Butch's receptive shoulder as they strolled down the road. Those sweet words were music to his ears as he put his arm around her tighter. The girl turned her face to him and her lips were inches from his, her sweet honey breath intoxicating as he gazed into those brown button eyes.

"I feel really close to you, too, Shirl." His fingertips touched the edge of her bra but if she noticed she didn't mind or pull away. He was in. Butch was thinking about how next week he would go for home base when the police car passing them slowed to a stop on the shoulder up ahead.

The Sheriff. Shit. He was getting out.

The knife. Fuck, they found the knife, Butch thought. He'd lost it and didn't know where, but everybody would know who that switchblade belonged to. It had his damn name inscribed on it!

Girdler walked unhurriedly up to Butch and Shirl, adjusting his shades and his Stetson. He tipped his hat to the couple as he approached. The boy realized he still had his arm around his dead friend's girlfriend so he quickly dropped it to his side.

"I'm sorry about your boyfriend, Shirley," Girdler said, sincere and firm. The girl smiled politely, eyes moist.

What was this about, wondered Butch?

"I gather you and Clyde had been together since junior high," said the lawman to the girl. They were real serious, she responded. Butch tried not to snicker, thinking about how Clyde had been sticking that thing of his in Annie, Carrie, Mary, Jamie, Sarah, Julie, Roberta and anything else in a skirt. Even his own girl

Joanne wanted to fuck that stud from the way she snuck slippery looks at him and she probably did fuck him for all he knew, the lucky prick. Not so lucky now. He was dead and Butch was glad.

He felt the Sheriff's eyes drilling into him behind the sunglasses, suspiciously sizing him up. Everybody sized him up. The boy felt the sudden need to piss.

"Butch, I didn't know you and Shirl was an item."

The kid had to say something. "Well, since Clyde and I was best pals, I'm trying to get Shirl over the hump is all."

"I see that."

"Is there a problem?"

"I don't know. Is there?" Girdler sort of smiled and Butch knew the man wasn't buying what he was selling. The cop took his eyes off the boy and put his hand on the girl's shoulder. "Well, Shirley, I just want you to know we're on the case, we have a few leads, and we're going to catch this guy."

Shirl thanked him and said it meant a lot. The lawman tipped his hat and walked away back to his car. Butch breathed a sigh of relief.

Suddenly, Girdler turned and looked laconically back at Butch. "Boy, you find that knife of yours yet?" Shirl looked at Butch, confused. Now Butch really needed to pee. The kid shook his head.

The cop got in his car and drove off.

"What knife?" Shirl asked.

losing the cell door behind him, Sheriff Girdler sat down and faced the dwarf. It was just the two of them alone in the police station.

"I gather there were hostilities between you and the dead boy the night of the murder," stated the lawman flatly.

"He was an asshole," grumbled the midget.

"Did you kill him?"

"If I killed every asshole there wouldn't be no folks left."

Girdler laughed. He took out his pack of cigarettes and offered one. "Got a point there. Smoke?" The midget took and lit a Marlboro Light. They both puffed in the holding cell. "What's your name?"

"Little Joe. I didn't do nothing."

"Who did?"

"How would I know?"

"One of yours?"

"You already asked me that."

"I'm asking again."

"Nobody in the carnival wants no trouble."

Girdler nodded and got up. He turned away from Little Joe and looked out of the cell, fingering the bars. "Listen, I get it," he said. "Your carnival is a family, a family different from other folks and a family's got to take care of itself. I know it must be tough for you traveling from town to town and I can't imagine the kind of shit you take from folks in some of these backward ass places. You carnival people got to stick together. You got to watch each other's backs. Who else would look after the alligator man, or that bearded lady, or even those twins?" The lawman spoke with genuine empathy and saw his good words getting through to the cagey carnie. "You got to protect one another, because if you don't, who will?"

"You got that right." The midget watched him, lowering his defenses a smidgen.

With that, the Sheriff swung around on the dwarf, leaning forward with both hands on the metal bunk on each side of the midget and fixed him square in the eye. "But there's something you need to understand, Little Joe. This town is my family and somebody killed one of us. Maybe the killer is somebody from my family or maybe from yours, I don't know yet, but you best believe I'm gonna get them. While I appreciate you people sticking together, I will keep you and your carnival buddies in town until you go out of business and end up on food stamps unless you folks open up and tell me what the fuck happened that night. Do we understand one other?"

Little Joe's eyes softened and he puffed smoke. "We do." With a sigh, the little person gestured for another cigarette and as the lawman gave him one and lit it, he told his story.

The night of the murder, Little Joe had run Clyde and Butch out of the Sideshow tent at gunpoint. He wouldn't have used the pistol. No need. They were just punks. Not like some of the white trash hard cases he ran into before. But those boys had been taunting the Geek, spitting on him, and the dwarf had gone to find Mr.

Stitch to get those little fucks thrown out, but when he came back with the manager, both boys were gone. Stitch figured they had just split. Little Joe knew better. Those kids were looking for trouble.

Somehow he knew where they'd be.

At the edge of the field there was a small tent over the back of a pickup truck. It wasn't one of the regular attractions. The carnies just brought certain locals there. Truth was, it wasn't exactly legal, which is why the midget hadn't told the lawman about it earlier. Those boys had found that tent. They could hear the clucking, the slashing and the squawks of pain. It wasn't like any sounds they'd heard before. Two muscular redneck carnies were guarding the tent over the pickup truck. The boys saw them and knew they'd have to sneak past. Candlelight shapes of several figures, some grotesquely distorted, looking down at something in some sort of pit, were silhouetted against the canvas. There was activity. Drops of blood splattered the canvas. Those punks snuck under the rusty back transom and crawled beneath the pickup truck to get into the tent. Little Joe supposed they probably hid there a while below the axle and the muffler of the vehicle, peering past the crates and straw, watching the spectacle.

For sure, neither of them had ever seen a cockfight before.

Two large battle roosters circled one another in a wooden stall, savagely hacking and chopping one another with their beaks. Blood and flecks of flesh flew. One of the birds had an eye out. Grisly feathers lay everywhere. The alligator man and the bearded lady were taking bets from a local gas station attendant named Franklin. The black rooster leaped onto the orange rooster and pecked its head until its skull cracked and brain and guano flew.

One bird lay dead.

A bottle of moonshine was passed.

The bearded lady flashed a winner's grin behind the huge forest of black fur covering her face, spilling over her fat breasts and floral print dress. She scooped up the money on the dirt beside the ring and stuffed it between her boobs. She retrieved the black bird and wiped the blood off with a rag. The alligator man picked up his prize rooster in scaly, leathery hands. A tear rolled down his reptilian skinned cheek. Carrying the corpse of his bird as gently as a dead pet, he put the limp mangled carcass in a wooden cage on the back of the pickup and closed the lid. The gas station attendant left, busted. That's when the alligator man saw the boys under the truck bumper and told them to come the hell out of there.

They did. The blonde kid asked if they had more birds. He wanted to bet and was an asshole about it.

"The young man had a name," interjected the Sheriff. "Clyde Dodd,"

"Right, whatever," said the dwarf as he continued with his story and told how the two boys had taken money out of their pockets, pooled their cash, and given it to the alligator man. It had been a slow night, which was the only reason the freaks had let the punks bet on the cockfight. Money was money. Usually, every place the carnival stopped, there'd be 5 or 6 guys from town betting, sometimes up to 25 if they were in the Deep South or near the Mexico border states. The money was good then. But these cockfights were illegal and risky and you could catch a big fine or jail time if the cops nailed you, even get their carnival license suspended. Plus, they were a pain in the ass to set up. Tonight, the boys were the only customers they had.

They both bet on the yellow rooster. The blonde kid figured the black rooster was tired. The other kid went along with it. The alligator man went to a crate in the transom of the pickup and brought out the yellow rooster, removing the headgear and claw gloves. He held it over the pit until the yellow rooster and black rooster were insanely snapping their beaks at each other's heads, ready to kill each other in the tawdry blood sport. They threw the birds into the pit. Both boys were savagely excited by the cockfight and cheered with every rip and tear of flesh and plumage as the birds circled and pecked to the death. That's when Little Joe came in the tent looking for Mr. Stitch and saw the boys. When it was too late to stop anything. In a flurry of feathers and gore, the squawking soon ceased and the yellow bird was now the red, dead, rooster. The black bird strutted, bathed in gore, ruffling its frill.

The boys were angry. They wanted their money back. They were told to go fuck themselves. The boys said the one rooster cheated and the freaks laughed. The boys said they would tell the cops about the cockfights and the freaks stopped laughing. Little Joe went to get Mr. Stitch, and that was the last he saw of the boys.

Or so he said.

A half hour later, Sheriff Girdler and Deputy Ross were at the carnival sitting in Mr. Stitch's trailer with Stitch, the bearded lady and the alligator man. Little Joe was in cuffs. Lots of cigarettes were smoked. The carnies admitted to running illegal cockfights and corroborated the midget's story about the chain of events with the boys.

But.

The boys left without incident.

"Can you prove that?" Girdler asked.

"There was witnesses." The alligator man croaked in a voice harsh as his countenance gotten from mass quantities of whisky and cigarettes.

"Who?" Ross asked.

"Those townies come right after Little Joe left," the bearded lady said indicating the dwarf. "Two from around here. Stayed for a few hours."

"Names?"

"They don't tell us their names."

"Descriptions?"

"One didn't have no left arm and the other had big ears."

"Tall and thin?"

"Nossir. Kinda fat and the one with the ears had no hair."

"Right, I was testing you," The Sheriff smiled wryly. He turned to his Deputy. "Sounds like the Dugans." Girdler flipped open his cell phone, eyeballing the carnies. "I call these farmers you say was here, they gonna tell us they was here that night and say they saw those boys leave?"

Stitch scowled. "We don't know what they'll say."

"Better damn hope for your sake that's what they say." Girdler dialed a number. It rang. Somebody picked up. "Rodney, its Danny Girdler. I'm fine, how about you? Rodney, did you see Clyde Dodd and Butch McCauley at the carnival the night of the murder?"

The freaks watched the lawman, exchanging furtive glances.

"You did. I see. Mind telling me where?" A pause. "Rodney, were you and Terry at a cockfight at the carnival? Listen, I'm not going to arrest you I just need to know if you saw those boys there. You did. Okay, what happened? Uh-huh. Uh-huh. Uh-huh. Thanks for your cooperation. No, we don't know who killed the boy yet. Yes, we have some leads. Give my best to your mother." The Sheriff hung up.

The apprehensive carnies looked at him nervously.

Girdler looked at Ross and nodded. "Take the cuffs off Little Joe." Then he looked at the carnies. "Your story checks out. The Dugans got no reason to lie." The Deputy unshackled the dwarf.

"You gonna charge us on the cockfighting?" Mr. Stitch asked tensely.

"Don't see how I can since as I just told two of my own citizens I wasn't going to arrest 'em for betting on it."

"Then can you let my carnival go and let us be on our way now?" Mr. Stitch faced Sheriff Girdler.

"When we catch the killer." The cops left the trailer.

After the door closed and the policemen were safely away, Mr. Stitch stepped away from the window and faced Little Joe, the bearded lady and the alligator man. Shafts of twilight from the shutters diffused through the cigarette smoke and dust in the trailer. The freaks faces were shadowed, strange, eyes glinting. The carnies exchanged conspiratorial glances in the darkness, a secret language between them. The carnival manager faced them. "Was that what happened?"

The alligator man drew a serrated Bowie knife from a sheath from his Frye cowboy boot and sat back, picking lint front his fingernails with the tip of the blade. A cigarette dangled from his leathery lips which were twisted in a sneer. "The pigs bought it, didn't they?"

Flick.

The knife glinted.

Flick.

Girdler told Ross to call it a night. It was dusk as they walked back to the fairground parking lot. The Deputy offered to buy the Sheriff a drink down at the local tavern. They were heading past the trailers of the carnies and Girdler looked over at a silver Airstream. Through the window saw twin female silhouettes of two women joined at the middle. Twin pairs of bras and lacey undergarments hung on a laundry line outside the trailer. He told Ross he would meet up with him later.

The Deputy needed that drink. After saying goodnight to Danny Girdler, he stopped off at the Deer Run, a local watering hole he frequented. The cop plopped himself on a stool at the bar and ordered a boilermaker. Feeling the good cool beer and sharp malt whisky was the prescription when he needed to get drunk fast. It got him there fast. By the third round, he looked away from the game on TV and saw the men. There were about 20 of them. Dodd was in the center. Ross watched the many heads hunched together, like a football huddle. He heard hushed whispers above the television game and commercials...

"Fairground..."

"Geek..."

"Grab him..."

"Do it ourselves..."

Draining his whisky, the Deputy thought fast. He needed to radio the Sheriff so they could stop this. Some of the men were looking at him now, rows of eyeballs from across the bar. Ross took a swig of the beer. That's what he would do. Call Danny. He took a nip of whisky. But there was no hurry. The men were just talking right now. He had time for another round. The mob of townsmen were getting up and paying the check. Ross' stomach tightened. He needed a drink before he called Girdler. There was time for another round.

The men began pushing through the door.

The Deputy signaled the bartender.

Sheriff Girdler sat in a kitchen chair in the Airstream trailer across from the two Siamese twin sisters in their jeans and tee shirts sitting at an adjacent angle on the built-in dinette. Coffee cups were on the table. Cigarettes burned in the ashtray. Sadie grabbed another two Marlboro Lights from the crinkled soft pack and girlishly stuck one in her mouth and one in Rose's. Rose lit it with a metal Zippo. They both saw the cop watching them and smiled sheepishly. He was charmed by them. "We keep talking about quitting," said Rose.

"It's hard 'cause each time we try, just one of us has a mind to. The second hand smoke gets the other started again," admitted Sadie.

Opening the high school yearbook, Sheriff Girdler opened it to the page with the photo of the young, beefy good-looking farmer face of Clyde Dodd. He wore a football jersey. "I hate to ask you again, but I need to know if you remember seeing this boy any time after he was in your tent during the night of the murder."

Two sets of eyes flickered as they studied the photo. The Sheriff watched their expression, but saw nothing indicating any recognition. Sadie looked at Rose. Rose looked at Sadie. Rose shook her head. Sadie shrugged, then shook her head, too.

"You sure?" He asked them. They both nodded, first one, then the other. The cop sensed a strong unspoken communication between the two Siamese twin sisters.

Rose gave Sadie a funny look. "Rose, can't you hold it?" Rose shook her head demurely. Sadie sighed. "Please excuse us."

Girdler watched as Sadie patiently got up and walked with Rose down the hall to the open bathroom door and went inside. The door closed, the locked turned and there was a sound of fumbling. The Sheriff felt uncomfortable yet curious wondering how the two sisters managed their bodily functions, then got his mind off it. Nature was a funny thing. Why should it make him uncomfortable?

He looked at a pinned, wrinkled Polaroid on the wall. The photo was of the two Siamese twin girls as children, 5 or 6 years old. They sat together on the floor of some room, sunlight streaming in through a big curtained window, backlighting them in golden halo. They wore one big dress, covering their physical joining. Both had beaming smiles on their faces, preoccupied with the dolls they groomed in their four hands, the girls' heads pressed together in a playmate intimacy of unconditional joy. They looked just like any other children.

The toilet flushed.

He was too busy looking at the photo to hear Sadie and Rose return. "That's us, but I guess you figured that, huh?" The Sheriff turned to see the twins standing behind him. Rose was gazing at the Polaroid with a sweet warmth and longing and spoke in her soft honey drawl. "Mama took that. Or maybe Daddy. I swear, we was so happy then. It was jus' me and Sadie and there weren't no world staring at us. Just us and the dolls. I swear we didn't know there was nothin' in the world but us." A peculiar peace and sense of loss flickered in Rose's eyes. "Wish me 'n Sadie we coulda stayed there forever 'n ever, Sheriff. We was safe." A tear welled in the gentle sister's eye. "I wish it had always been just the two of us."

Sheriff Girdler watched her and understood. In that moment he felt a sudden wrenching compassion for the girls.

"You want to see the dolls, Sheriff? We still got 'em." Rose started for a cupboard by the trailer kitchenette that had several old rag dolls.

Sadie touched her sister's arm, tossing her hair coquettishly. "Now Rose, don't be simple. The Sheriff is a busy man and he's our guest and he don't got no time to be looking at silly dolls." She smiled, her lipstick glinting in an awkward, saucy charm. Rose, Girdler noticed, did not wear any makeup.

Surprised by his affection and fascination for the two human oddities, who were so human at the same time, the

Sheriff found himself disarmed. "Why that's just fine, Sadie. I don't mind. I'd love to."

Rose beamed, warming to Girdler, trusting him. She walked with her acquiescent sister over the rag dolls with lace dresses and porcelain faces and button eyes on the counter. "This one here's Rebecca. She's the younger one and she always needed to have her hair braided 'cause it got to be a mess."

The cop picked up the doll and admired it to Sadie's coy embarrassment but Rose's shy delight.

"And this one is Betty," Rose said picking up a larger antique doll. "She's always up to no good."

"Those are beautiful dolls."

"Why, thank you," Sadie said.

Girdler noticed there were identical stitches on the sides of the two dolls the same place that the sisters were attached. It was as if somebody had sewn them together then changed their mind and took them apart, stitching to repair the damage. He was about to ask about it but thought better of it. Suddenly uneasy, the Sheriff grabbed his hat.

"Well ladies, thank you for time. And the coffee. Now either of you remember anything else, you call me day or night. Here's my card. Got the office and home number on it." Girdler dropped his card on the counter of the dinette and crossed to the door.

On his way out, he saw the two Siamese twins silhouetted in the window.

"You come by any time now," they said in harmony. Four hands waved.

The cop walked across the grass to his car, feeling a strong sense of unease in the carnival shadows lengthening through the midway attractions. This place was just different, and wrong. Now, he just wanted to get out of there and get home. So Sheriff Girdler swung behind the wheel of his car and sped out of the field back onto the main road.

Many eyes were watching him go. The men moved through the bushes. Ernie Dodd was in the lead. He carried a rope. He carried a cloth. The mob from the bar carried baseball bats and brandished bare fists. A few bottles of whisky glinted.

The Sideshow tent lay ahead in the shadows and moonlight.

Girdler drove down the highway to town and rang his Deputy. He got no answer, so, a few more miles down the road, he rang him again. Ross still didn't pick up. That wasn't right and wasn't like Ross.

His house was just a mile south so Girdler figured he better check in. He drove there but the lights were out and Ross' car was missing. Girder turned his Plymouth back towards town. As he did, he rang up the Deer Run. The bartender answered. "It's Danny Girdler, Wallace, looking for Ross. He there?"

"He was, Sheriff. Left about fifteen minutes ago."

Slamming on his brakes, Girdler screeched the car to a sudden halt.

His Deputy stood in his headlights on the side of the road, blinking. It looked like he had just been walking there, clenching a bottle of booze. Shocked, Girdler leaped out of the car and confronted Ross, who swayed on his feet, drunk off his ass.

"What the hell is wrong with you, Ross?"

"Can't a man get drunk?"

"What's wrong?"

"Nothing. They're going to kill the Geek is all."

"*Say what?*"

"Danny, I was at the bar. A bunch of boys from town are heading out to the carnival. They're liquored up. They have weapons. It's Dodd. He got 'em riled."

"How long ago did they leave the Deer Run?

"20 minutes."

"You knew this and didn't radio me?"

Ross mumbled.

"Answer me you drunken fuck!" Girdler grabbed him by the collar and heaved him against the car. "Why didn't you radio me?!"

"What good would it do?"

"We stop 'em is what good it would do. We're the law. Why didn't you—?"

"I don't know."

"Sober up. They're probably at the carnival by now. Sounds like a lynch mob. We get over there fast maybe we can stop it." The Sheriff rushed over to the driver's side of his vehicle, but the Deputy backed away from the car, shaking his head and shivering. "Get in the damn car!" Girdler yelled to Ross.

"No."

"Now!"

"No, Danny. It's the whole damn town!"

"That's a direct order Ross. Get in the car."

"I-I can't."

The Sheriff felt a white-hot rage and pointed at the useless Deputy. "You're fired, Abner! You hear me? Fired! I want your badge and gun on my desk tomorrow morning!"

Ross waved him off drunkenly, staggering away down the roadside darkness. "Asshole!" Girdler yelled. Alone and outmanned, the Sheriff leaped behind the wheel, slammed the door, threw on the siren and the party lights, and blasted a hairpin U-Turn back up the road toward the twinkling carnival lights.

Ross was showered with gravel as the red auto taillights receded, their simmering glow fading over the dismal and miserable sodden wreck of the Deputy. Stumbling, he lost his grip on the whisky bottle, which fell to the ground and shattered on the side of the road. The wretched man dropped to his knees, bent over and started to cry, his fingers clawing the gravel.

Something metallic gleamed on the ground.

He knew what it was even before he grabbed it.

They threw the rope over the tall branch.

The other end was a noose tight around the Geek's neck.

"We're gonna do this nigger style!" Ernie Dodd roared.

The freak, roped and hogtied, squirmed and struggled against the sweating bodies of the lynch mob that held him firm. He saw the lights of the carnival and safety miles away in the distance. They had driven him way out into this dark field in the middle of nowhere. That was after all those men had ducked into his tent and captured him in his cage, tied him up and gagged him, and then loaded him in the back of a truck and stole him from the carnival. While it was occurring, the Geek didn't know what was happening, but knew it was bad. Now he knew what was happening and it was as worse as it got.

Dodd got in the pathetic creature's face, shining his flashlight. "You killed my boy, you fucking freak, and you're gonna pay. Pay with your life you sack of shit. You'd never get the death penalty. No lethal injection or chair. Not in this day and age. Some shit ass bleeding heart would cut you slack because of the way you look. They'd lock you away or maybe even just put you in a hospital and you'd probably like that. All shut away nobody making fun of you. Hell, they wouldn't even rape you in prison looking like you do."

The Geek blubbered. Its eyes were wide and lugubrious with fear and pain. Dodd's satisfaction faded as he saw the freak's pain.

"You don't even understand a word I'm sayin' do you?" He spat in the Geek's face. Then he turned to the men and walked away. "String him up."

Headlights exploded over the scene. The lynch mob whirled at the sound of screeching tire rubber. Red police cherry-tops ignited the blackness. A car door slammed open.

"*Dodd! What the fuck are you doing?*" Sheriff Girdler stepped out of the shadows and into the headlights, fiercely backlit, a pump .12 gauge shotgun gripped in his fists. He was all by his lonesome.

Dodd stepped forward, pointing at the crumpled freak. "That *thing* killed my boy!"

"We don't know that."

"Look at him."

"I am, and if this is what it looks like you boys are in a world of hurt."

"Sheriff, I best believe you best back off." Dodd advanced, emboldened by booze and fury.

"What did you say?" Girdler saw things spiraling out of control fast.

"You heard me."

"I'm the Sheriff."

"Not here. Not tonight."

The Sheriff's stomach felt like a rat was running around a wheel in it, not even aware of himself cocking the shotgun and injecting a cartridge of buckshot into the breech. "I'm not going to tell you again, Ernie. Step back. All of you. *Now.*"

The bodies of the mob closed ranks behind Dodd. This was a very dangerous situation and somebody was going to be dead before it was over. The air smelled so strong of alcohol Girdler figured if he lit a match there'd be an explosion. Even now, the scene was Hell without the flames. Girdler looked left and right at the raging, whisky fueled distorted faces of the 20 townsmen gathered around him. He felt a few bodies step behind him. Boots cracked on twigs. The cop moved in a slow 360 with the shotgun, finger on the trigger, and saw he was surrounded. This was surreal. Blood was in the air. Sanity had slipped. What was he going to do, shoot them? He'd never seen any of these people like this and he'd grown up with them. Familiar faces at the Elk Lodge and Lion's Club.

But these faces were different.

They looked like…

Freaks.

Dodd stepped forward, full of false courage. "You work for us, Sheriff. We pay your salary."

"Right, know what that means?" Girdler grinned.

"What?"

"I have the authority to lock all your sorry asses up."

Nobody laughed.

"How many shells you got in the Remington, Danny? Five maybe. There's twenty of us. Think about it."

"That a dare?"

"How many shots you think you'll get off before we overcome you?" Dodd licked his lips. Girdler now saw hesitation, from fear or conscience, on a few of the faces. He felt the cold sweat between his hands and the metal of the gun making it slick and slippery. "Anything happens to you and the freak and it's our word against yours. But maybe you won't be saying much." The Geek, rope noose around his neck, cowered by the tree.

Somebody was going to die.

"You know something, Dodd, you're right." Girdler had made up his mind. "I don't need this shotgun." He dropped the gun.

And hit Dodd closed fist in the jaw so hard he heard it break.

The men jumped back. The Sheriff kneed Dodd in the groin, dropping him to his knees. The embittered father slumped to the ground, gagging as he tried to rise. Girdler kicked him again and again in the ribs. Rogers, the butcher, and Franklin, the owner of the gas station, tried to pull him off Dodd but he struck them, pushing them off.

The lawman was screaming at the top of his lungs. "Look at what you done, Ernie! What's wrong with you? What's wrong with all of you? I don't recognize any of you? Who are you, boys? I don't know any of you anymore! Look at yourselves! You're acting like fucking animals! Nothing but a filthy bunch of animals and freaks! You hear me? *Freaks!*" The Sheriff whirled around on all of the stunned townsmen now coming back to their senses. "Now get the fuck out of here, all of you, before I change my mind and get my shotgun and put all you *freaks* out of your fucking misery!" The outraged Girdler rode the wave of violence pouring out of him, surprised that he never knew it was there.

The lynch mob, cowed by the cop's raw, righteous fury, backed away. Girdler stood gasping for breath, eyes wild, his chafed and bleeding fists clenched. The circle of bodies around him slowly disbanded like a loosening garrote. Shadows of the townsmen, shoulders slumped, retreated to their cars.

"And take this sorry ass with you!" The Sheriff grabbed the limp Dodd by the scruff of the neck and heaved him towards the others. Two men picked up the broken down old Coach and loaded him in the car with them.

They all drove off.

Sheriff Girdler crouched beside the Geek. The freak was crying. "I'm going to take you home now," the lawman said quietly.

Moments later, the cop drove silently down the empty stretch of blacktop. The Geek sat in the vinyl backseat, huddling in the gloom. It sang a nursery rhyme to itself in a surprisingly gentle voice. As he sped into the darkness, Sheriff Danny Girdler felt as alone and strange as the freak in the backseat. It would never be the same in the community again. Not with these people, not after tonight, and where he would go from here? He didn't know. Tonight, Girdler had stood alone against the town and felt completely cut off from humanity, the people he had faced having no recognizable human traits. Through the windshield, the car plunged into endless country darkness. As dislocation and oblivion embraced him, and with it an overwhelming sense of being down a road he could never turn back on, it felt good to have someone, anyone, in the car with him. A fellow traveler on that same dark road with no way home.

Suddenly, the Geek spoke. "Thanks," it said.

The carnival lay ahead. It had started to rain, hard.

An hour later, Girdler was home in bed when the phone rang. Ex-Deputy Ross's voice was agitated and excited. "Been trying to get hold of you."

"Be sure your badge and gun are on my desk in the morning."

"I found a knife."

Girdler sat up.

Ross continued. "It was lying on the side of the road near the fairground. It has the name 'Butch' inscribed on it. Danny, I dusted for prints."

"What part of your ass is fired didn't you understand?"

"It's got Butch's fingerprints on it."

"Blood?"

"Some. I'm dropping it off at the medical examiner in the morning to see if we get a match to Clyde." Girdler sighed. Telling Ross he was fired was like abandoning a hound dog you've had for years on the side of the road and expecting it not to follow when you walked away. Plus, his Deputy's voice made him feel a little less cut off from humanity. "Want me to pick him up?" asked Ross.

"I'll do it in the morning. He's not going anywhere."

"Danny, I'm real sorry about tonight. I just want it to be over. For me. For you. For the Dodds. For this town. Hell, Danny, I'm even starting to get some sympathy for those freaks."

"Yeah, me too."

"See you in the morning, then?"

"You're still fucking fired."

"I know."

Sheriff Girdler slammed the phone down. He lay back in bed and rubbed his eyes. He lay awake for long moments listening to the storm outside as he pictured Butch McCauley knifing Clyde Dodd before the relentless patter of rain on his room lulled him into sleep.

He had just dropped off when he got the call.

"Sheriff?"

Fumbling with the phone, he immediately recognized the soft nasal twang. "Rose?"

"Come over." Her voice was a barely audible whisper.

"What's wrong?"

"Come over. Now." Her usual lazy drawl was breathy and swift, so low he could hardly hear it.

"Speak up Rose, I can hardly hear you." The cop looked at the clock on the bed stand. It was 3:19 AM. He rubbed sleep from his eyes and sat up groggily.

"Sadie's sleepin'. Can't wake her. Need to talk to you now. Be real quiet, Sheriff. I left the door open for you 'fore we bedded down."

"Can't it wait until tomorrow?" From the urgent tone in her voice, he already knew it couldn't.

"No Sheriff. Come over. I don't tell you now I'll lose muh nerve."

"Give me ten minutes."

"Be quiet. Don't make no sound when you come."

Girdler hung up, tugging on his pants.

The headlights of his car flared the bushes on the driveway to the fairgrounds. The Sheriff shut the lights and realized he could see enough by moonlight to drive. Looming shapes of the Ferris wheel and carousel, the trucks and the tents, rose out of the darkness like an alien planet. The carnival Sideshow slept. Ahead, around a bend in the muddy road, he saw the bullet shape of the silver trailer of the Siamese twins. The cop, mindful of Rose's admonition for quiet, parked several hundred yards away behind a canvas awning. What could she want? It had been on his mind the whole drive through the deserted Alabama Route 12 roadway. He'd heard something troubling in the tone of her voice. Something that must be heeded. His shoes crackled on twigs in the mud as he made his way across the fairway to the Airstream. Girdler had just thrown on a denim jacket over his jeans and realized that his skulking figure could look suspicious.

The trailer was dark. It was silent. Testing his foot on the metal ladder he took a step with no creak. He reached out slowly and touched the button handle of the rickety door and it swung open.

Unlocked.

All of sudden, he wished he brought his gun. Entering the womblike enclosure of the trailer, he looked right and left. The kitchen was dark and still, dishes in the sink, dappled with moonlight from the window. In the other direction, the narrow and claustrophobic hallway led past the bathroom and pantry to the open rear door of the Airstream bedroom.

"Sheriff?"

It came from in there. A whisper so soft he almost didn't hear it. Instead of answering, the cop slowly, soft footed made his way down the black corridor. He couldn't see inside the bedroom yet because his eyes were not accustomed to the dark, but with each step his vision grew clearer until at last he made out the two big lumps on the mattress. There was a slight metallic creak of spring suspension on the trailer as he walked to the doorway of the back of the trailer.

"Shhhhhhhh." Rose had her finger to her lips, watching Sheriff Girdler a few feet away. She lay in bed beside Sadie, who snored loudly beside her, sound asleep. They both were clothed by the single big nightgown with two collars they wore to bed. The awake sister's eyes were button wide as she gestured the cop beside her.

Figuring he did not have to do the talking, Girdler carefully eased down on one knee by Rose's side of the bed, following her gesture for him to put his ear by her lips so she could whisper.

"I gotta whisper so's Sadie don't wake. She won't want me telling you this."

The Sheriff felt the warm, sweet breath of the Siamese twin's full lips brushing his ear and the room was full of the musk of the two women he could see were naked under the dual nightgown. Beside Rose, Sadie's leg was spread and her gown was hitched up over a bare buttock, smooth and shapely to the dark hair between her legs. She snored.

Rose whispered as quiet as a mouse, her drawl tremolo with fear and apprehension.

"Sadie killed that boy."

Girdler held his breath, turning his head a smidge to see Rose's eyeball huge by his, her lips brushing his cheek, as she lay attached to her sleeping twin. "Tell me," he whispered. "Everything."

Their faces touched, and he felt her hyperventilating breath as he was frozen in place on one knee beside the bed in the warm, close funk of the sister's room. And, not moving a muscle beside her Siamese twin fused by a rope of flesh and organ a foot away, she confessed.

The boys had both had a lot to drink when they came to the trailer for the first time a week before. Clyde was the more talkative, aggressive one. Butch was at first shy, but after a few more beers he started to unwind. They wore varsity jackets and had tight jeans. They were football players and both Rose and Sadie knew this type of kid and usually stayed clear. But they had money.

And both wanted to fuck a pair of Siamese twins.

Afterwards, when the boys went outside for a smoke break, the two Siamese twins struggled to roll onto their back and lay naked on the mattress, bathed in perspiration.

"Did you like it?" Sadie asked.

"We didn't do it. Butch couldn't," Rose admitted.

"I popped my cherry and you didn't?"

"I'm kind of glad. I kind of didn't want to."

"It hurt."

"It looked it."

"In a good way."

"Did you like it?"

"Rose, I want to do it again."

"You do?"

"Clyde is mine."

"Okay."

"You can't fuck him."

"I wouldn't want to."

"Promise."

"Promise."

"We gotta wash these sheets, there's blood on 'em."

"I think those boys run off."

They heard raised voices outside, arguing. Naked, the conjoined sisters lifted themselves on their haunches, sitting their bare buttocks down on their heels as they faced one another. Sadie took a handkerchief and dabbed away the blood in between her legs. Rose grabbed another tissue and reached gently between her sister's open legs and winced. Their faces were close, gaze soft and intimate.

"You okay, Sadie?"

"Rose, I ain't no girl no more." A smile like a boa constrictor snaked across Sadie's face. They both started to laugh girlishly, embracing one another.

The voices outside grew louder. The twins peered through the trailer window. Shirtless, Clyde was outside getting in Butch's face. Or it was the other way around. They faced one another angrily.

"Pussy, you couldn't do it!" Clyde yelled at Butch, who turned his back and stormed off, shoulders slumped in shame and defeat.

Moments later, they heard the Airstream door creak open. Seconds passed. A fumbling in the pantry. The sound of the refrigerator opening. The clink of cans and the pop of one being opened. Then Clyde staggered into the rear bedroom, bare chested, his pants unbuttoned, he leaned against the doorway clutching an open can of beer. The boy took a swig, staring lasciviously down at the naked Siamese twin sisters on the mattress.

"Hey," he said.

"Hi," smiled Sadie, eyelids fluttering.

Rose didn't say anything. She didn't like the way he was looking at her and her sister, but mostly at her. Or the way his pants were tightening at the crotch.

"Pussy went home to Mommy. Boy didn't know what he had," Clyde chuckled, rolling the perspiring ice-cold aluminum beer can across the roped muscles of his sweating chest, grunting in tingly pleasure. "More for me." The boy had a bad look. "Just us now." That look was directed at Rose. "Your sister was tight. You as tight? I wonder if yours is tight like hers bein' as yer twins 'n all." He rubbed his bulge. "I'm up for another round. How 'bout you?"

Sadie looked nervously at Rose, who avoided Clyde's gaze, so Sadie turned to the boy and made bedroom eyes.

"Sure, 'cause you're so fine 'n all."

The randy young man sat on the bed between them. He put hand on Rose's breast and fingered the soft boob. She was too scared to budge. The boy stared predatorily into the virginal twin's eyes as his hand found its way down her bare belly past her navel into the forest between her legs.

"Get off my sister, you sumbitch!" Sadie screamed, her face all twisted up like a harpy as she pushed Clyde off the bed. Rose was shocked by the hideous, jealous expression her sister wore.

The rowdy boy rose to his feet, pants around his ankles, drunk and laughing. "Hey relax baby, you two do everything together, right?" Then he was back on the bed, hands all over Rose who tried to push him off, but he restrained her, shoving his tongue in her mouth. "C'mon, baby you know you want it!"

Sadie was screaming in hysterical fury, beating and scratching Clyde as he forced himself on Rose. The sports star used his athletic knees to pry open her sister's closed legs as he reached between his legs to stick it in her. Rose thrashed and desperately resisted as the football player wrestled with the two conjoined girls and physically overcame them both.

"You're mine! You're mine!" Sadie shrieked. "Stay off my sister or I'll—"

Then Clyde was screaming.

Rrrrrrrrip.

Then he just gurgled.

Rose saw there was a lot more blood on the sheets than before, and it was getting bloodier every moment. Drenched with splatters of spraying red blood, the grisly switchblade gripped in Sadie's fist was plunged again and again into Clyde's face. The knife sheared the skin off his forehead, opened the flesh of his cheek, exposing the skeleton of the jawbone, and hacked off his nose as the blade blurred through the air like a red tooth. Rose was tossed to and fro as psychopathic Sadie used both hands to drive the switchblade into Clyde's head and shoulders in a bloodthirsty, feverish rage.

Staggering to his feet, bleeding like a steer, the teenager had a moment of true terror realizing his handsome face had been ripped off and that he had been mutilated and disfigured beyond repair. More so, he realized all that blood everywhere was his. But it was all over quick, as Sadie had buried the switchblade in Clyde's gut, and when she pulled it out, part of his pink intestine came along with it. After that, his limp body slid down the wall and crumpled to the floor.

The Siamese twins sat on the bed, covered head to foot in blood like a modern art sculpture. Their eyes were white and wide in their red, red faces. Rose looked over at Sadie, in a state of shock, holding the knife. She softly pried it from her fingers and put her arm around Sadie, hugging her gently. Then, slowly, Sadie put her arm around Rose and hugged her back as Rose started to cry. The tears washed streaks of blood away from her cheeks.

It was late and the carnival was asleep. After they had cleaned up the trailer, the Siamese twins had carried the body to the river and dumped it. They watched it float downriver. They had bathed naked in the cold stream, washing one another tenderly in the dim moonlight, looking like fairy tale nymphs to any observers. But there were no observers. They washed off the blood, washed off the sex, washed off the tears. They washed themselves clean.

That had been two nights, three hours and fifty-one minutes ago.

Sheriff Girdler finished listening to the story, his stiff neck cricked from leaning down with his ear to Rose's lips.

"And that's what happened, Sheriff," the twin breathed in a hushed whisper. "Swear every word is true. Haid to tell someone. Haid to."

All he could do was nod. The rain was coming down in a drenching flood that rattled the aluminum siding of the Airstream trailer. Girdler sensed she was done, and very slowly, so as not to made a sound and awaken Sadie, he turned his entire head to face Rose and the tousled hair of the Siamese twin sister behind her.

Sadie's huge, enraged blue eye was bulged open!

Her face was pointed towards them, listening to everything. Sadie suddenly let out a hideous high-pitched shriek and grabbed something from under her pillow that flashed metallically in the moonlight. *Click.* A Smith & Wesson .38 Special revolver. Hammer thumbed back, Sadie pressed the gun muzzle to the temple of her Siamese twin's head.

"Cunt! Cunt! I'll blow your head off, cunt you cunt!"

The lawman leaped back, jumping up on his feet in shock and horror as Sadie used her body to heave Rose's torso and hips into an upright sitting position, the awkward action caused both sisters to cry out in pain from the strain on their congenitally fused spine. The cop reached instinctually for his belt but there was no gun there. It was back in the car.

"Don't!" was all he could say. The sight before him was grotesque and unnatural, both Siamese twins resembling some bizarre mythical creature, joined by flesh at the hips, one with a pistol to the other's trembling head. Sadie's and Rose's faces were Greek drama masks, one of terror, one of rage. Sadie firmly gripped her sister around the breasts with one arm and savagely clenched the .38 to her sibling's skull with the other. Her finger was itchy on the trigger. Rose struggled in raw panic, kicking with her legs and knocking the bedcovers askew as Sadie swung her own legs to the floor using the edge of the mattress for purchase. The pistol toting half of the Siamese twins used her hostage sister as a body shield, stumbling off the bed and dragging Rose to her feet.

"Let me go, Sadie!"

"I'll shoot you, cunt!"

"Please don't hurt me!"

"You told him!"

Four feet hit the floor.

Sheriff Girdler showed his empty, open hands to Sadie peering over Rose's shoulder with a crazed stare as she backed away down the hallway. "Don't shoot. I'm unarmed."

"You stay back, Sheriff. I know how to use this."

"I'm sorry Sadie, I had to tell somebody I had to."

"I'll deal with you later, cunt!"

The cop held Sadie's gaze, watching the girls' retreat, watching the barrel of the gun aimed over Rose's shoulder and aimed between his eyes. "Sadie, you know I got to take you in. You know you got to give up."

"No way."

"Sounds like this whole thing maybe wasn't entirely your fault. But you got to turn yourself in and let the law handle this."

"That's a fine joke, Sheriff. We gonna get a jury of our peers?"

"I swear you will get treated fairly."

"Treated fairly?" Sadie spit in disgust. *"We're freaks, ain't we?"*

The watchful Girdler took a careful steps towards them, hand out.

Sadie screeched and the gun swung towards him, freezing him in his tracks. *"Stay back! We're getting outta here!"*

"Where to? Think Sadie. Where're you gonna run?"

But then the sisters were gone and rain was rushing through the swinging, creaking metal door of the trailer. The two conjoined female shadows had bolted out the trailer door and he was alone in the close air of the RV.

The rain was coming down dark and heavy, turning the ground to mud as the Siamese twins lumbered down the steps of the Airstream trailer. Sadie was dragging her hostage sibling at gunpoint, their bare feet splattering the mud, two unnatural silhouettes in the shadows of the fairway. Lightning struck. Girdler burst through the door of the trailer, squinting in the frigid, rain swept darkness to spot any movement at all amidst the antediluvian shadows of the sleeping carnival rides. He winced as his face was pelted with stinging drops, soaking him. "Rose! Sadie!"

Then, in a staccato electrical blast of lighting, he saw the fleeing shadows dart behind the Ferris wheel.

Leaping off the Airstream platform he made a dead run through the pouring rain for his parked car, cursing the distance away he had left it. He had to get to his gun. The mad sister was armed and even though he doubted she would shoot Rose, he didn't know anything about Siamese twins and wasn't sure what they would do. Where the hell did they think they were going? As he reached the drenched Plymouth, slipping in the sloshing mud, he at last threw open the door and got his hand around his holstered Colt Python .357. They didn't know where they were going, they were just getting away.

But Sadie had a gun and somebody could get hurt.

Girdler suddenly realized he didn't want either of those girls harmed.

So it was going to be up to him to disarm them.

And as he moved out into the labyrinth of storm swept carnival rides, he knew this was the girls' turf, not his own.

Four nipples showed under the single wet nightgown that was all that clothed them. The drenched, muddy wrapping looked like statue marble over the four legs, four buttocks and the flesh bar of physiognomy that interlocked their hips. Twenty toes stumbled through the sludge. Rain poured out of their mouths and streaked their hair into their eyes. The Siamese twins sought refuge behind the Merry Go Round. Sadie was gasping, keeping the pistol barrel jammed against Rose's head.

"We gotta give up!" Rose pleaded.

"Hell you say!" Sadie hissed. *"There he is."*

Sadie peered down the gun sight of the pistol at the small silhouette of Sheriff Girdler ducking through the erector set framework of the Loop The Loop. Rose cringed, staring at her sister's gun arm outstretched next to her ear. Sadie closed one eye, taking deadly aim. The single notch of the barrel lined up with the dual notches on the breech on the stick figure of the cop just as a strobing charge of lightning ripped the world.

Sadie pulled the trigger.

As Rose grabbed the pistol hand with her own, yanking hard and throwing off Sadie's aim.

Sheriff Girdler winced as the slug exploded on a steel beam a few feet away, showering sparks as it ricocheted into the mud. He saw the flash of the gunshot almost at the same instant as the bolt of lightning. Then he made out the violently tussling twin shapes by the Merry Go Round, swirling like attached double shadows. Grabbing his gun, he fled the cover of the Loop The Loop and ran into the torrential rain in a dead heat for the carousel. As his feet pounded the mud, and he closed in on the struggling Siamese twin sisters, he saw two faces contorted in emotion as four hands grappled for the gun. The struggle etched in the staccato flashes of lightning. The pistol fired again. And again. A slug whistled past his shoulder. Then he was on them. His outstretched fist closed on Sadie's wrist, tossing away his gun so he'd have two free hands to grip hers with, then Rose seized Sadie's arm as well. Sheriff and sister both knocking the gun hand against the steel frame of the ride. With a dismal cry of despair, Sadie's fingers unclenched and the .38 dropped from her palm into the mud with a splat. The Sheriff kicked the pistol safely away under the carousel. In one swift move, his right hand swept to the handcuffs on his belt and he snapped one manacle over Sadie's wrist, hooking the other on a metal eyebolt.

And it was done.

The Siamese twins slumped in the mud and pouring rain, soaked and filthy, dangling by one arm handcuffed limply to the carousel. The Sheriff stood over them grimly as thunder sledgehammered. The girls' downcast faces stared at the ground, hair matted to their features.

"You have the right to remain silent," he began softy. Girdler sensed the presence of other bodies appearing in the rain, their sadness and fear tangible as they kept their distance. Surely this rain would never end, he thought, as he read the sisters their rights and arrested them.

People were strange fruit indeed.